ANNA POLITKOVSKAYA:

NO
TO FEAR

ANNA POLTKOVSKAYA:

NO
TO FEAR

DOMINIQUE CONIL

Translated by ALISON L. STRAYER

THEY SAID NO SERIES EDITOR, MURIELLE SZAC

Triangle Square Books for Young Readers
Seven Stories Press
NEW YORK • OAKLAND • LONDON

Seven Stories Press
www.sevenstories.com

Library of Congress Cataloging-in-Publication Data

Names: Conil, Dominique, author. | Strayer, Alison L., translator.
Title: Anna Politkovskaya : no to fear / Dominique Conil ; translated by
    Alison L. Strayer.
Other titles: Anna Politkovskaya. English
Identifiers: LCCN 2022011290 | ISBN 9781644211304 (hardcover) | ISBN
    9781644211311 (ebook)
Subjects: LCSH: Politkovskaia, Anna--Juvenile literature. |
    Journalists--Russia--Biography--Juvenile literature. | Women
    journalists--Russia--Biography--Juvenile literature. | LCGFT:
    Biographies.
Classification: LCC PN5276.P64 C6613 2022 | DDC 070.92
    [B]--dc23/eng/20220511
LC record available at https://lccn.loc.gov/2022011290

Cover illustration: François Roca

College professors and high school and middle school teachers may order free
examination copies of Seven Stories Press titles. Visit https://www.sevenstories.
com/pg/resources-academics or email academics@sevenstories.com.

Printed in the USA.

9 8 7 6 5 4 3 2 1

To Nina

Thanks to Michel Parfenov
for his attentive rereading

"Words can save lives."

ANNA POLITKOVSKAYA

Contents

1

"Her Name Is Anna Stepanovna Politkovskaya"

"Her name is Anna Stepanovna Politkovskaya, she's at the university studying literature and journalism. Her husband too," Seryosha had said. "She really insisted on meeting you . . . Yes, I know, she's from the *nomenklatura*,* the daughter of a diplomat, but you'll see, she's different . . . Anna Stepanovna Politkovskaya, you'll remember the name?" Finally, sighing, I said yes. Seryosha is stubborn, and he'd brought me half a pound of fragrant coffee, a rarity found only in stores for foreigners.

---

* In the USSR and the countries of the former Eastern Bloc, the most trustworthy members of the Communist Party, and generally those who enjoyed special privileges.

That is how I've come to be here, on a Sunday in February 1979, between the concert hall and the statue of Mayakovsky.* It's the kind of Moscow winter day I love, the kind that never quite seems to begin and gently dies with the afternoon. Cars and pedestrians are rare. From time to time, a figure darts to the kiosk and then disappears behind the statue. A great silence hangs over the city, the snow falls in big flakes; everything is muted.

I don't hear her approach. Suddenly she is there, slender and running . . . right past me. A married woman, she? Surely not! More like a boyish young girl. I see her slip on a pair of glasses: she simply hasn't seen me. Too short-sighted . . . And it's true that our Soviet glasses are not the most flattering.

But with or without glasses, with a fine wool shawl wound around her head, hunched under one of those heavy Soviet coats, she is very pretty. A long fine-boned face under light brown bangs,

_____
* A great Soviet poet.

the look of a girl from another era, one might say: glowing skin, shoulders speckled with snow, a slight rounding of the cheek. She reminds me more of an old-fashioned dreamer than a Soviet journalism student during the period we call "stagnation"—that says it all!

And Anna, what does she see? An old man, probably . . . though I'm only thirty-seven. I, Vassily Pachoutinsev, *chapka* tugged down over my eyebrows, not very clean-shaven, pant legs rumpled and sagging over thick and solid leather boots. A dissident,* as I was labeled by the director of a French magazine that published my stories, which took a very ironic view of our regime. In other words, an evil spirit, prone to criticism. And so a dissident I became! I was summoned to the bureau of the KGB,** our

---

* In the USSR, the term was used for intellectuals who contested the regime. They were severely persecuted during the Soviet era.
** Secret police and political intelligence service (now called the FSB).

omnipresent police force, and for a few months I brushed up against serious trouble—it's forbidden to publish abroad without permission. I lost my teaching job at the university . . . and got by with the help of my friends. One found me translation jobs that allowed me to scratch out a living; another managed to pull a few strings so I could keep my home.

But it's not the dissident Anna Politkovskaya wants to meet.

"Let's walk a little," I say.

In the Soviet Union, when we want to be sure not to be heard, we walk. We get very used to talking in temperatures of five degrees.

"I brought you a gift," she says, handing me a book that has obviously been read and reread.

And it's a wonderful gift: an American edition of the poems of Marina Tsvetaeva, impossible to find in Moscow. That's when I ask her to come to my home. The trust between us is immediate, total, and inexplicable.

"Is it wise to be writing a thesis on Tsvetaeva? Not the surest way to get a good grade . . ."

I'm intrigued. Marina Tsvetaeva was never one of our "official poets." She wouldn't be one of "our poets" at all if, after her death in 1941, her daughter Allia hadn't fought and talked her way around the censors for years to publish a handful of writings. People clamored for those books, but there were so few of them . . .

And now this young woman is preparing a presentation on Marina Tsvetaeva at the risk of failing her exams or becoming very unpopular. She asked to meet me because I helped Allia, before she died, to sort out some of Marina's papers, and so I was able to read poems that few people know of.

When we come out of the metro at Tretyakovskaya station, the snow crunches under our feet. In a low, soft voice, she talks about Marina, her independence of mind. Anna has the polite manners of a well-bred child and follows me down the crowded hallway of the communal apartment.*

At my place there are little piles of books everywhere, but I can't complain. The apartment is right in Moscow, not in some distant low-rise building. It has a very high window looking out on the trees in the courtyard and, when it doesn't snow, the green roofs on the opposite side. Anna asks me questions. She listens so carefully that I get over my shyness. She sits on the floor, jotting down notes. We pour more tea . . . and time moves on.

This is my first meeting with Anna Politkovskaya. When she leaves—"I'm late! I have to pick up my son from my mother's!"—I watch her go. Sliding more than walking between the snowdrifts in the courtyard. I remember that she told me she was a good skater and had even been invited to join the national team of young hopefuls.

---

* After the revolution of 1917, large apartments were requisitioned to house many families at once, each given one room to live in, with a communal kitchen.

Her eyes shining, she also told me about Sasha, her husband.

I see some similarities between this young person and the poet. Like Marina, she wants to hold on to only the most intense moments of life. And like Marina, she takes off her glasses, even if it means seeing the world as a great blur.

A few months later, she calls me. The dean of the university didn't say a word during her exam, but in the end, it went well. She has the self-assurance of an excellent student.

"And what are you going to do now?"

"I'm not sure . . . journalism . . ."

Much less sure of herself!

2

Daughter of *Perestroika**

How dreary everything is in the early 1980s!

And it seems as if it will never end. Our leaders look as rigid and frozen as the mummy of Lenin in Red Square. Yet there are things that I like about this life.

Sometimes I wait at dawn in front of a bookstore where we know such and such a book is about to arrive. A small group of fans, usually under observation by the gentlemen of the KGB, we stand in a tight circle trading *samizdat* books—novels, stories, or poems that are typed, copied by hand—outlawed, secret. Each book is a treasure.

---

* "Reconstruction," a reform movement initiated by Mikhail Gorbachev in the mid-1980s.

We wait in line for hours to buy theater or concert tickets, and the emotions we feel stay with us for months.

And money doesn't really exist. Not having any doesn't change much; in fact, the shops are often empty!

Later, no one will miss the narrow apartments without refrigerators or IKEA furniture, but we have so little that we share a great deal. Everything in our Soviet world is absurd—shipments of padded coats that arrive in the summer; the "chance" of getting meat that was bought who-knows-where, cut up in a bathtub, and delivered around in a rattletrap car— so we laugh a lot. You might as well.

Also, when the new General Secretary of the Communist Party Mikhail Gorbachev talks about *glasnost** ("transparency") and *perestroika* ("renewal"), we couldn't care less. It's just more

---

* Another movement initiated by Gorbachev: freedom of expression and an end to censorship.

hot air . . . But I begin to understand that something is changing when I watch *Vzgliad*, which would translate to *Viewpoint*, on TV! It's a real shock, for the whole country.

Every Friday night, neighbors gather at my place to watch *Vzgliad*. And it's like that everywhere! Music clips, skits, but most notably, for the first time, an explosive team of young journalists who cover all the banned subjects: the Stalinist deportations, economic collapse, freedom of expression, homosexuality. They fly off the handle, shake up solemn people who've never seen anything like them before. And all of it live on television! It's as if they are lifting off the lid that is suffocating us.

Anna's husband, Sasha, a tuft of hair sticking up from his forehead, with his bright eyes and quick comebacks—a kid from the suburbs, bold and brash—is one of the stars of *Vzgliad*. So popular he's going to be elected a people's deputy!

Anna works at *Goudok*, the transport newspaper. I think she must be bored there. Later I will learn that she took advantage of the free plane tickets to explore the enormous USSR . . .

One day in 1988, I get a phone call. Would I agree to appear on *Vzgliad* the following day? They are going to talk about banned poets. I have to elbow my way through the crowd in front of the television building in the Ostankino district. People are pushing and shoving each other to get into the recording studio, and up on the blue-lit set, it's hardly any different. Between the cables, dozens of people are standing around— musicians, gulag survivors, and the director of a Red October factory, women who've come with baskets from their market gardens in Crimea . . . And Anna, sitting a little behind them, with that good-girl look about her.

"Do you work here?"

"No, television doesn't really appeal to me. Sasha loves it. But I believe in the power of words."

However, as I become a regular at their tiny apartment on Herzen Street, I quickly realize that Anna truly does participate in *Vzgliad*. Sasha has a way with words and takes a lot of risks—he even goes down into the Chernobyl reactor*— but it is Anna who finds the forgotten letter in his pocket: a woman writes that at the hospital in Minsk, Belarus, children who have been exposed to radiation are dying for lack of care. It is Anna who sends Sasha to film the story. And rejoices when equipment and medicine arrive. For her, the purpose of journalism is not only to inform; it's also a lever for change. This idea never leaves her.

During this time, Anna is often radiant. In love with Sasha, in love with her children, Vera and Ilya, swept up by the euphoria that has taken hold of us all. There is nothing left in the stores, our economic system is collapsing, our wages arrive after months of delay, but that doesn't stop us!

---

* On April 26, 1986, one of the reactors at the Chernobyl nuclear plant in Ukraine exploded. It was a major disaster for the environment, especially in Ukraine and Belarus.

The word on all our lips is *choose*: our lives, our shoes, our political party—everything. I sometimes wonder if the lid will fall back down. But Anna is a daughter of *perestroika*, she believes in it. We spend entire afternoons talking. She tells me about her childhood in bits and pieces, the life of a Soviet princess— the good bilingual school, the music lessons—and that of an enthusiastic Pioneer* and diligent reader at the Krupskaya library.

"And then there were the other books . . ."

Posted at the United Nations, her father brought back books unknown or banned in the Soviet Union. She devoured them all. "That kind of freedom has no price," she says. We laugh a lot. Anna's laugh is really something, explosive and contagious. "My Cossack laugh,"** she says. And a Cossack she is, a direct descendant of the famous rebel warrior Mazeppa! _

---

* The Pioneers was a youth organization whose goal was to create good young Communists; membership was obligatory between the ages of ten and fourteen.

** Cossacks are a people of southern European Russia and adjacent parts of Asia, distinguished as cavalrymen, especially during czarist times.

Maybe I'm a little in love . . . Oh, from a distance, without really believing it. Some days I go with her to get Ilya and Vera from school, and I'm amused to see the rebel instantly transform into an anxious mother who is even a little severe. It's out of the question for the children to play in the yard with friends, even if they are dying to do so. Everyone gathers around the piano that stands in the middle of the living room. Compulsory music. Ilya sighs, Vera grabs her violin . . .

For several days, a rumor has been going around Moscow. There is going to be a bloodbath. People "in the know" say there will be firing on the crowd.

Usually that's enough to discourage people. Everyone stays home and thirty brave souls go out and get arrested.

But today, the incredible happens. Walking hand in hand, Anna and I merge with a tide of people that sweeps across the city. Everyone holds hands. Anna wears her funny cap, which gives her the look of a street urchin, like Gavroche in *Les Misérables*.

We haven't seen anything like it in Moscow for seventy years! We're not afraid anymore.

It's bitterly cold but no one cares. On this February 4, 1991, we don't want much and yet what we want is enormous: Article 6 taken out of our constitution, the article that gives the Communist party the exclusive right to rule our lives. A few months later, when everyone has fled the oppressive heat of Moscow, tanks converge on the White House, the seat of the Russian parliament. It's the beginning of a coup d'état, instigated by "hard core" Communists, who reject change. On all the television screens, a big loud-mouthed guy harangues the crowd with "Let's defend our freedoms!" It's Boris Yeltsin. Anna, vacationing on the Baltic Sea, jumps on the first plane home, as do many others. She will never forget these moments, the Russian people defending their newfound freedom.

But I'm worried. Something is coming to an end, but I don't know what.

3

Listen to the People

"I was force-fed politics! For years! And that's all Sasha talks about. So I've had it up to here with politics!" Anna says decisively.

"You know what they say. If you don't take control of politics, politics takes control of you . . ."

It's been a while since I've seen her because I've started working with the Memorial Society,* founded by former dissidents. We gather information and documents on millions of Stalin's victims. At a time when so many luxury shops

---

* An NGO dedicated to human rights founded in 1988 by academician Andrei Sakharov. The Memorial Society was involved in the opposition to Putin and the war in Chechnya.

are opening, we don't miss a chance to say how ridiculous we are and how we must look to the future and not the past. But people are growing old and dying; photos are lost, memories fade. So it's a matter of urgency, and Anna agrees.

Besides, when it comes to human rights our work is never done. There are always battles to fight. Soon Anna and I will be working side by side, she listening to a woman with a distraught face while my eyes flit down a list of names.

All is not well in Anna's life. When the deputies rebelled against Boris Yeltsin, now head of the country, the army was sent out after them . . . Sasha did everything to prevent them from being shot, but in vain. There were I-don't-know-how-many deaths, and since then, Sasha's career has been on the decline. People in high places don't like him very much.

It didn't take him long to become a star, and it hasn't taken any longer for him to become an out-of-work journalist. *Vzgliad* has disappeared.

And the phone doesn't ring very often on Herzen Street.

Anna who once raged, "I can't move ahead! He takes up the entire road!" is now worried. Sasha stays out late with friends and drinks too much. She bangs the pots and pans, gives more music lessons, writes more articles, and works late into the night. In her newspaper, which emerged from *perestroika*, she covers "social" issues.

The foreign press loves to describe Moscow's mutation. The old neighborhoods with their hodgepodge buildings are being expropriated to build high-rises and shopping malls, or luxurious villas surrounded by high walls. The "new Russians." The limousines you see in the streets now. They write about the powerful mafias, gangland killings, and incredible fortunes built in a few months thanks to oil, gas, and banks . . .

But Anna writes the other side of the story. People who are evicted from their homes. Children in remote and impoverished republics who are brought to Moscow and put to work as slaves. Pensioners and unemployed engineers selling their last possessions on the sidewalks. Patients who can no longer receive care in the impoverished hospitals. She listens, asks questions, grabs her phone, and harasses authorities. Demands explanations, from clerks all the way up to ministers.

The Anna who's had-it-up-to-here-with-politics is not yet famous, but she's one hell of a hard worker. I begin to admire her precise and lively writing, her way of keeping the reader's attention with the most everyday misfortunes, the fight in her when she goes after the people responsible. Gradually, I get in the habit of sending people to her. Her way of sitting down on a sticky bench in an asylum, leaning forward so she can hear more clearly.

While oligarchs* organize lavish parties with

---

* A category of businessmen with ties to the political regime. With the low-cost purchase of state-owned enterprises, huge fortunes were made under Boris Yeltsin. The same process continued more quietly in the entourage of Vladimir Putin.

4

"How Can They?"

"Come look."

Anna doesn't even turn. She's in her usual position, chin in hand, eyes glued to the television screen. Next to her, a mug with two tea bags steeping at once, and at her feet, Martin the dog.

On the screen, I see something I'd hoped never to see again: Russian tanks advancing, shooting.

I do mean Russia, since we aren't the Soviet Union anymore and haven't been for several years. Ukraine, Belarus, and the Baltic countries became independent first. We haven't gotten used to it. It feels strange, as if we've shrunk.

And now there's our army on its way to a "quick and victorious" raid in Chechnya, as

Yeltsin announced. In front of the tank on the television, a half-destroyed building. "Grozny is about to fall," the commentator says.

"They're bombing civilians," says Anna. "How can they?"

If there's a people that doggedly desires its independence, it's the Chechens. Since the time of Peter the Great. Starting in 1991, Chechnya has declared its independence, without asking Moscow's opinion.

"The Chechen rebellion is in its last days," trumpets the TV commentator.

"I doubt it," says Anna.

Rape, torture, massacres, abductions. Half the capital destroyed. Civilians are already paying. The war becomes a quagmire, Yeltsin resigns. Nobody sends Anna to Chechnya, and she's still chomping at the bit.

5

"Leave Chechnya Immediately, or It Will Never Leave You"

"Planirovka! Planirovka!" A rallying cry announces the editorial conference where the issues of the day are discussed at the *Novaya Gazeta*. And in the hallway where everyone is heading pell-mell for the big windowless room, Anna gives me a high-speed update on her life: she and Sasha have separated, she has now joined the staff of this little independent newspaper that is becoming one of Russia's last bastions of freedom of the press. And she's thriving! At the newspaper, some are young, some older. There are violent clashes. Less than modest salaries. But this motley group becomes strongly united as soon as one of them is attacked. And it happens often.

More than a decade later, in 2011, entering the *Novaya Gazeta* is like entering a small fort. At the front door to the anonymous building, an armed guard stands near the walk-through security portal. Six of *Novaya Gazeta*'s journalists and close contacts have been murdered since 2000.

But in September 1999, people come and go as they please, and Anna invites me to stop by and see her. She is so full of energy, while Russia is so tired . . . the country yearns for safety.

The great bank crash of 1998 ruined millions of people. Chechnya is in a state of great upheaval.

Faced with a demoralized and angry country, Boris Yeltsin once again changed the prime minister. This time he chose a little cold-eyed gray man whom many believe is short on personality: Vladimir Putin.

Personally, I'm leery of the little gray man, former head of the FSB, which is no longer called KGB but is still the same powerful police and intelligence service. Anna feels the same way. And suddenly, in September, things start happening more quickly.

We are stunned by a series of attacks. For two weeks, in Moscow and elsewhere, powerful bombs explode in apartment buildings, killing nearly three hundred, injuring thousands. Incredulous, we look at the gutted facades, the speeding ambulances. Immediately, the Chechens are accused.

It is then that Prime Minister Putin announces that they'll pursue Chechen terrorists everywhere, and "waste them even in the outhouse." This manly expression is his, not mine!

And in Grozny, all hell breaks loose. Bombs rain down on the capital, already very damaged by the First Chechen War.

"I'm leaving," Anna tells me at the end of the month over the phone (it's a bad connection). "I'm going to Chechnya!"

"I'll go to the airport with you," I say.

She drives like a snail, cautious to the extreme, and now on the road to the Domodedovo airport we have the same kind of traffic jams as Western countries do. Night falls, Anna doesn't say much. She leans her cheek against the glass. Grave. In her thoughts, she's already gone. Yesterday she told her editor Dmitry Muratov: "I want to go to Chechnya." She heads to the counter, gives me a casual wave, and pushes her way through the crowd.

A few days later, passage to Chechnya is blocked. Only two or three journalists left in time to get through. Others are stranded at the border. Putin, the little gray man, understood one thing. As he likes to say, "What we don't show doesn't exist." So journalists have to choose. Either they follow the army and only see what officials want to show them, or they stay where they are, on the other side of the border.

At first I have no news from Anna besides a short call: "I'm okay."

My friend Tania, who went there during the first war, keeps repeating: "You know, either you leave Chechnya right away, or it will never leave you."

The bombing of the capital, Grozny, is unrelenting.

One evening, Anna calls me.

"You get here and you think you're watching an American action movie. And then you realize that no, it's real. And frightening."

Then . . . the line is cut.

The following day I read in the newspaper what happened next. In 2003, Grozny will be given the sad distinction of "the most destroyed city on earth."

Anna is there with the locals. Everyone's misfortunes—those of men, women, children, the elderly, Chechens but also Russians, caught in a war that is beyond their comprehension and that many didn't want—that is what she talks about.

How people live under fire, with the whistle of bullets, the deafening roar of low-flying planes, the burning buildings. People huddling in basements, away from the walls, running under fire when it can't be avoided. How quickly they run out of everything—water, electricity, food. She talks about the long trails of refugees on the roads who are sometimes bombarded. "Why is this happening, if it isn't to destroy a people?" she asks. She talks about their arrival in peace zones, where they are cooped up in camps, completely destitute. She chronicles how suspects—and all Chechens are potential suspects—are interrogated, tortured, and shipped to detention centers from which they often don't return.

She is caught up in the misfortunes of those who remain behind, unable to imagine that their doors will open, that soldiers will enter and shoot them. Something resonates in every article. Anna observes, accosts military officials—from draftees to generals.

I'll tell you a little story:

Anna hears about a nursing home, right in Grozny, where two hundred elderly people have been totally abandoned. Thirty are bedridden. The staff have fled, terrified.

Anna goes after the people in power who, suffice it to say, are not easy to track down. To her it seems more urgent to save than to write. Everywhere she speaks out on behalf of these elderly men and women, demanding that they be evacuated. She asks them all, the Chechen authorities, the Ingush and Russian ministers, and nobody does anything . . . If she is thrown out of an office, she goes back the next day.

Meanwhile, as it is, between fires and famine, the elderly population is dwindling. So Anna writes an article, reporting everyone's names and their answers, the broken promises and indifference. A little later, she has to write a second article. The day before, a Russian minister boasted of having saved the nursing home, and the Chechen rebels, to prove he is lying, take the unfortunate old people hostage . . . Anna spares neither the rebels nor the minister. The story causes such a sensation that the elderly people are finally saved . . . just before a bombing.

In both articles, Anna cites some thirty names to pin the blame on. But how many enemies has she made? I'm worried about her.

And I'm right to be worried. The *Novaya Gazeta* receives thousands of letters, subscription cancellations, and insults! The Russians don't want to hear about this dirty war. Or rape. Or looting. Or summary executions. Or destroyed villages. They want peace and order, and Chechnya is far away.

Upon her return, Anna is exhausted but by no means overwhelmed. On the contrary.

"I've never felt so sure about what I'm doing," she says, "despite all the horrors there."

She moves into a sunny apartment on Lesnaya Street and becomes a mother who's always on the phone. Ilya complains too, he's afraid for his mom.

As Sasha will later say about Chechnya: "Anna got up on a furious horse and never got down again." It's funny, she never takes off her fine-framed glasses anymore. She has to see everything.

Now that she's back, she re-learns everyday life, goes to the gym, the hairdresser, writes at a comfortable desk, but a part of her is always "back there." Then a phone call comes. A desperate, exhausted voice; or the whisper of an official who can't take it anymore, or a soldier who wants to confide in her. She leaves again.

Vladimir Putin clamps down on independent TV stations, which will either no longer be independent or will disappear. One by one, the newspapers are starting to filter information, as in the past. Everything is fine! Voices like Anna's are few and far between. This is what connects us.

From time to time we meet to listen to music—and these are thoughtful and quiet evenings—but often we're side by side with the

Committee of Soldiers' Mothers, who fought so long for the withdrawal of Russian troops from Afghanistan in the past, and from Chechnya today. Anna knows what people mean when they talk about young Russian soldiers in muddy boots, exhausted and mistreated, driven to cruelty. And while there are some mothers who insult her by mail, others in distant provinces who receive the sealed coffin of their son who died in battle think that the only way of finding out what happened is through her.

Anna is not a war reporter. The uniform really doesn't interest her, though she loves the state of emergency in which people find themselves in wartime, making every encounter intense.

But thanks to her, "refugees"—those anonymous, dirty, and ragged people, all crowded together—one by one recover a name, a face, a job, a life story. The old man lying prostrate in a caravan who begs to be allowed to die? He is an honorable professor at the Institute of Petroleum who has trained generations of engineers. Anna manages to find his son and save him, but never again will he see the forty thousand books in his burned library. The girl of great beauty, who is dying after a dozen bullets were shot into her body, once again becomes the spirited and confident student of literature she was two weeks earlier.

During the worst times of the war, Anna never forgets the humanity of a Russian officer trying to feed people with broth, or the courage of a soldier who whispers to a woman to hide instead of killing her as he's been ordered to do. People, all of them . . .

"Anti-Russian"? Her articles often end with questions. What do we do? How are we to act? And it's we, the Russians, for whom the questions are mainly intended. We, the Russians, who were so freedom-loving only nine years ago. And in our country, where great violence goes hand in hand with great acts of generosity, some people read the articles of this peculiar journalist.

6

Nord-Ost

Nord-Ost is everywhere! In Moscow, it's the runaway hit of the year. All the teenagers I know want to see this musical extravaganza.

October 23, 2002. The play is in its second act; a troop of uniformed soldiers frolics on stage. The huge theater is packed. Whole families with children and teenagers have come to see this show with its touch of Soviet nostalgia and breathtaking special effects.

Playing in the orchestra is Kostya, a friend of Anna's children, Vera and Ilya. He too has been devoted to music from an early age and is making his debut with *Nord-Ost*.

Suddenly the actors fall silent. Kostya, in

the orchestra pit, can't see what's happening onstage. The conductor freezes and the young man stands. Hooded people, women with veils draped close to their faces, belts of explosives around their waists, push the actors aside. In the silence, a man grabs a microphone.

The Moscow theater hostage crisis begins. The man at the microphone demands the withdrawal of Russian troops from Chechnya.

Kostya watches the members of the commando—some forty people—installing wires and explosives. There is panic in the room. Ninety people manage to escape through the emergency exits. For all the others, the wait begins. I try to reach Anna. Answering machine. I suddenly remember that two days earlier she left for a faraway destination.

She's in the middle of a reception . . . in New York. She, who has so often written that this savage war leads to terrorism, is receiving the Courage in Journalism Award. She's starting to become a celebrity! Two years earlier, while investigating in a small remote village near a Russian military base, she disappeared for three days. Informed of the disappearance, the *Novaya Gazeta* alerted the international press. Certain important people made very official inquiries about what had happened to her. And she was released, after a mock execution and threats. That day, she most certainly escaped death.

Igor Domnikov, a few months earlier, was not so lucky. He was investigating corruption and was murdered by hammer blows. Domnikov was the first journalist *Novaya Gazeta* lost. He was forty-two, the same age as Anna.

At the theater, some hostages are released. There is no food or water. The young veiled women, their belts of explosives around their waists, whisper to their neighbors in the theater that they have nothing to fear. Some of the hostage-takers are teenagers.

Anna flies to Los Angeles. She plans on spending a few days with friends in California. But an Aeroflot plane comes to get her, it's an emergency; the commando wants her to act as an intermediary. Oh, it wasn't easy. To start with, President Putin's entourage refused—anyone but her, they said!

I wait for her near the theater in a small and worried crowd that the special forces and police are keeping at a distance. I see her arrive, very pale. She has come straight from the plane.

Kostya tells me later about sitting in the orchestra pit, thinking to himself that he was too young to die, he hadn't even made a record . . .

A murmur goes through the ranks of the hostage-takers: "Anna's here, Anna's here . . ." The only one they trust.

Anna Politkovskaya comes back out, knowing there's a way to negotiate and probably obtain release for everyone. She says so. Insists. The authorities don't respond. The decision to attack has already been made, but we don't know it yet.

Then I see her from afar, carrying packs of bottled water, many packs. The police stop her. She explains, and returns to the theater with the water. I wave.

"That's all they'd let me do, bring water," she says, dropping into the seat of my car.

She trembles from fatigue, cold, fear.

"I was terrified," she whispers. "Those hundreds of coats hanging in the coatroom. The darkness. And silence."

Arriving at Lesnaya Street, we hear on the radio that another small group of hostages has just been released. Anna makes one phone call after another. She hits a brick wall.

We know what happens next. At dawn a toxic gas is diffused throughout the theater, putting people to sleep, but also causing brain hemorrhages and irreversible internal damage. Special troops enter and shoot all the sleeping kidnappers in the head.

Kostya, ill but a survivor, sees the special forces men, with rough and careless gestures, heap up the bodies of people who had been watching the play. One hundred seventy people died, including one hundred thirty audience members. Others continue to suffer the aftereffects.

Anna denounces the rigidity of Vladimir Putin, the use of a deadly gas without telling the powerless rescue workers what it was or what was in it. Families wander from hospital to hospital in search of their kin.

We are devastated.

"Anna," I say, "you have to learn to be careful, really."

She smiles her new smile, which is a little sad. "The best way to be careful is to not give in. To continue my work."

What can anyone say to her?

In Russia, people approve of Vladimir Putin, who was elected president in 2000. Here is a man who doesn't let himself be pushed around. Hundreds of TV spots feature him as a superman hunter-fisherman-diver-aviator-warrior who hobnobs with the political elite and organizes grand ceremonies. Anna has hardly any influence, but her fame spreads abroad. Her articles are translated, collected in books. The better known she is elsewhere, the more of a disturbance she is here.

7

Her Name Was Elza

Will he be up to the task, this young Stanislav Markelov? A brilliant lawyer, not even thirty, and ready to do battle with the Russian courts to obtain justice. I look at this too-thin redhead coming up the path to Memorial, and ask the question out loud.

"Yes," says Anna. "He's very good."

Sitting side by side on a bench, exchanging looks, she in her long coat, me in my thick jacket, we must look like a team of tired detectives. We're working closely on this case. In the three years that Elza Kungayeva's peaceful gaze has met ours whenever we open the file, we've suffered a number of defeats. Anna has written a great deal. She's the one who started it all.

In the village of Tchangi Chou in Chechnya, people were frightened of Colonel Budanov, a career military man, always ready for a fight, depressed, a heavy drinker. On that day in 2000, he headed into the village to do battle, drunk and determined to flush out terrorists. But in the house he entered there was only a girl. Regardless, they abducted her on the colonel's orders; she was taken to the hovel he occupied, and he shut himself up with her.

When the body of Elza Kungayeva was found, doctors concluded that she had been beaten, raped, and strangled. Is it necessary to point out that Elza had nothing even remotely to do with the rebels?

"What do you call killing people because of their ethnicity and that alone? I call it genocide," says Anna.

From the beginning, she pursues the story.

First the courts find no great harm; then, when people protest, they say that Colonel Budanov can't be condemned. Because he's "crazy," not responsible. And so they mean to put him away for a while and release him quickly.

"These courts remind me of others that took orders from the government—Stalin's," writes Anna. "They refuse to hear witnesses and judge as they are told to by people in high places." Then Stanislav Markelov has the idea of asking for independent and foreign experts to be brought in to assess Colonel Budanov's mental health . . .

Today, we are waiting for the results and Stanislav's return from Tchangi Chou. Elza's parents, simple but determined people, continue to struggle. German psychiatrists have come and made a report and create a scandal in the Bundestag, the German parliament. And suddenly, everything is overturned . . . the colonel is condemned.

Vladimir Putin, "although he doesn't give a damn about the opinion of his countrymen, attaches great importance to criticism against him abroad," writes Anna, riding on the strength of this victory.

Now, as I write this, I know that death isn't far away for me. I find it hard to walk. My breathing is labored. I spend more time on the chair near the window. I don't get bored, I think back on those who've been important in my life, on important moments; it's a film that I can replay a thousand times. Even though there is more sadness in it than anything else. One night during the time of Budanov's trial, our young Stanislav was severely beaten by unknown assailants. All they said was not to deal with people from the Caucasus anymore.

In February 2009, Stanislav Markelov, thirty, lawyer for human rights and the *Novaya Gazeta*, would be murdered as he came out of a press conference.

As for the liberated colonel, he would be walking in the Moscow Gardens in June 2011, when he, too, would be shot.

It's a strange film, playing back again. Sometimes I'd like to leave it on pause.

At the *Novaya Gazeta*, some people have had enough of Anna Politkovskaya. They tell me, I sense it. Scathing and at the same time fragile. Besides, she's not the only one working on incendiary topics! Yuri Shchekochikhin, in 2003, pays with his life, poisoned, within a month of starting a corruption investigation. Again investigating corruption, he dies of poison within a month. Everyone misses his warmth and good nature. While Anna, obsessed with Chechnya, obsessed with Putin, is possessed of a personality that kinder people describe as "difficult."

"Why don't I like Putin? I don't like him because of his cynicism, his racism, his lies," she writes ten, a hundred times, and sometimes too hastily, according to Dmitry Muratov, the chief editor. This is the source of their epic battles, the throwing of various objects followed by reconciliations . . . She is invited overseas more and more often, but on her return, I frequently find her discouraged. Oh yes, she is held in the highest esteem, put up in the best hotels, and people love to get their photo taken next to Anna Politkovskaya, but when it comes to condemning human rights violations in Chechnya or Russia . . . not many politicians do it anymore. Trade contracts, oil and gas purchases come first.

8

Death at School

For us, the first day back at school is a gala affair. It's called the "Day of Knowledge." Of course, it's a legacy of the Soviet era, but we like it very much. It's always jolly. You see it on an amateur video shot in Beslan, a midsize town in Ossetia, a small Russian republic. Girls with huge brightly colored ribbons in their hair and new dresses, music and laughter, some kids with their parents, a cheerful and chaotic scene.

The video suddenly ends there. A moment later, as children, parents, and teachers arrive at the school, a truck pulls up and thirty men get out, masked and armed. Fathers and teachers intervene. They're killed on the spot. So are the two women in the commando . . . They protest that children should not be taken hostage.

More than twelve hundred people are crammed into the small brand-new gym. No water, no food. Mothers with babies they brought with them when they accompanied their older children to school.

Meanwhile in Moscow, the press is rushing to cover the story. All the journalists, Russians and foreigners, are clamoring to get on planes for Ossetia. I call Anna: I'm sure she's on her way, if not already there. Her voice on the phone echoes in the hubbub of an airport.

"We're all stuck here," she says, "flights are delayed, delayed . . . I have to go, I've got a message . . ."

Around her people are stamping their feet, loudly complaining, calling their editors.

We don't know it at the time, but her cellphone is permanently tapped. A man approaches: there's a flight to Rostov that leaves in a few minutes. Rostov is not Ossetia, but Anna thinks she can find a way to get to Beslan. She runs down the tarmac. She has a message that the separatist president Aslan Maskhadov wants her to deliver, imploring the commando to release the hostages. The group includes Chechens, of course, but also Islamists from other places. Would the commando have listened?

We'll never know.

Once inside the plane, she orders tea. Takes a sip and immediately feels very sick, has just enough time to make one last call to Dmitry Muratov—"They've poisoned me"—and falls into a coma.

Meanwhile, in Beslan, the twelve hundred hostages are growing weak and dehydrated. It is very hot. Mothers with babies are released but must leave their older children behind. Around the school, the local people wait. Often armed. The commando calls for the withdrawal of Russian troops from Chechnya.

We don't know who sparked the first explosion inside the school. According to Russian authorities it was the commando. According to the surviving hostages and external witnesses, it was the Russian special forces. The attack lasts eight hours while fire destroys the building. Local firefighters don't have the equipment to fight it.

At least 344 people are dead, including 186 children, and more than 500 injured.

In Rostov, the doctors' quick reflexes save Anna Politkovskaya's life. Only just. She is brought back to Moscow, very weak. For three days nobody phones or is given any news, except for those very close to her . . . fear has returned.

Stop, I tell her. Enough is enough. She has a beige blanket wrapped around her. Her complexion is chalky. She can hardly eat anything. Whispering, she says no, because that would mean fear has won. I have to bend down to hear what she is saying.

9

No One Is a Journalist in Their Own Country

"Anna Stepanovna, how many years have we known each other?"

She stretches. Around us, the motionless silence of the late-summer countryside.

"A long time, Vassily Ivanovich . . . You knew me at nineteen, just married . . . You're talking to an almost-grandmother!" And she laughs.

I gaze at her with the tenderness of a grandfather and old partner-in-crime and friend . . . a scarf tied around her neck, perspiring, a spade and a basket of carrots under her arm. A far cry from the impeccably groomed Anna Politkovskaya with earrings and the serious, almost icy demeanor that most people know.

Up until now, Anna loved coming to the *dacha*,* but without showing any great interest in gardening. All it took was for her daughter Vera to announce that she was pregnant for Anna to transform into an organic vegetable grower and enthusiastic grandmother!

She kneads the long ears of van Gogh, her "charity case" dog.

"Vera will move into Lesnaya Street to wait for the baby," she says.

Van Gogh rests his sad gaze upon her. This good-sized bloodhound, only just adopted, has become a four-legged problem. He is afraid of everything and everyone. Trembles at the prospect of going out in the street, and tries to hide behind Anna's legs, fleeing fellow dogs and peeing at the drop of a hat when worried, which is often. Anna was advised to get rid of him.

---

* A *dacha* can be a shed in nature or a luxurious villa, but it is always out of town. Most city dwellers have a *dacha* where they can grow a few fruits and vegetables.

"Wash my hands of him, certainly not," said Anna, "I don't give up."

Bees gathering pollen swarm around the entire length of a tree, the buzzing never stops, and I tell myself that Vera's future baby will get something from Anna that no one has managed to get until now. Some peace and quiet, a little room for good times.

Everything is difficult. Rumors are going around about Anna, spread by the reporters whom she doesn't hesitate to call docile servants of the Putin regime. It is said that people have died because of her, have been murdered after talking to her. It's happened, we both know. But Anna and I also know that everyone's silence would be worse. She is no longer invited to press conferences at all. She is banned from television.

Not long ago Dmitry Muratov spoke sharply to her.

"You have to look things in the face, Anna. The

Chechen rebellion is crushed, or almost, Vladimir Putin has appointed one of his own men, Ramzan Kadyrov, as head of the country, and, increasingly, people are too scared to talk to you."

"We know why. The kidnapping and torture continue. I can't give up now . . ."

"Stay on the sidelines for a while. Write on safer subjects."

And again she said what she so often says: "Words can save lives."

And look at her now, talking about hospitals, birthing, carrots, and grains. But I know she's always there to listen, and if she is doing fewer investigations at the moment, it isn't because she's given up. She's not going soft.

Moreover, she has published a portrait of the young tyrant who is the head of Chechnya. She describes him as a psychopath, at once terrible and ridiculous. We know that Ramzan Kadyrov is furious at her depictions of him.

That day at the station, Anna waves goodbye with sweeping gestures. On the train, I have the feeling I'm being followed. I probably am. But it's a beautiful day, the people around me are bringing home their summer treasures, armfuls of flowers, bags of canned food for the winter, their skin reddened or tanned from sun, and at station stops they good-naturedly fend off the swarm of women who come onto the train selling trinkets made in China.

I never see her again.

10

To Die in October

In September, Raisa, Anna's mother, thinks she'll be in for two or three hours, no more. A routine checkup, one of those obligatory medical exams that cut into your day. Tall and slim like her daughters, Raisa is aging beautifully. But that day the doctors come back to her with grave looks on their faces. They have to operate, and fast. There's no way she's going back home.

She calls Stepan, who arrives right away. The two have been together for fifty-four years, and love each other just as much as they did in the days when they won dance competitions—tango, one of Anna's favorite kinds of music. Stepan offers to bring Raisa what she needs from home, says he won't be long. On his way back to his beloved, he collapses in front of a kiosk. Heart attack.

In a few hours, everyone—Elena, Vera, Ilya, Anna—agrees to say nothing to the patient, and invents a story to tell her instead. The family pulls together and gets organized. Anna phones me: she won't come see me this afternoon as planned because she's going back and forth between the hospital and the funeral home. There is so much to do that she hasn't even had time to mourn her father. This is one of those moments where life and death collide.

In Russia, we have a custom for mourning. It is said that the soul of the deceased doesn't leave us for forty days. It hovers around, and we gather together and bid it farewell. On October 7, Anna instructs Vera to eat a special breakfast for expectant mothers, and talks at length with her sister Elena.

Then she rushes to the hospital, where her mother's heart gave out the day before and her condition is still worrisome.

She calls Ilya, there are plenty of errands to run and groceries to carry; can he come and give her a hand for the mourning vigil?

She calls the *Novaya Gazeta*, her article is almost finished and she'll send it in the afternoon. She goes to the supermarket.

She returns, driving like a snail. As Dmitry Muratov would say, we sense when we're being watched or followed. Yes, it's true. If Anna didn't notice anything, it's probably because she had other things on her mind: her father's death, her mother's operation, her daughter's child.

On the security footage, you see the shadows behind her at the supermarket. In front of the camera at her building, we see Anna carrying her packages, and the backs of two people.

Two men. Who fatally wound her and finish her off, professional-style, with a bullet in the head. A neighbor discovers her body in the elevator shortly after. Meanwhile, *Novaya Gazeta*'s deputy editor, Sergei Sokolov, is trying to reach her. The cellphone rings in a vacuum. Ilya, who

11

A Legacy of Courage

I know a lot happened in the days that followed. Ministers and presidents spoke. Rallies and demonstrations took place in countries around the world. Many articles were written.

Forgive me, at the time I was grief-stricken. There was anger in my sorrow. I went to the *Novaya Gazeta*. The atmosphere was studious, concentrated; people talked in low voices. Tons of flowers had been left on the landing, in the hallway, on Anna's desk. With a jerk of the head someone indicated Dmitry Muratov's closed office door. In a moment of despair, he'd wanted to shut down the newspaper. What's the point of continuing—so that people get killed? The team's response was to publish a special issue on Anna, hastily put together, full of emotion, rage, and solidarity. Like everyone else, thousands of people, I went to her funeral. In the coffin, death gave her a stern nun's face, very beautiful, but not her. The dean of the university said she was the pride of Russian journalism, the same dean who'd remained silent when she defended her thesis on Tsvetaeva. In my mind I saw the snow-covered girl sliding between snowdrifts, a book under her arm.

And then one morning, I went to the Ribni Torgovi fish market. I stopped, stunned. Anna was everywhere, on the cover of every newspaper. She was all you could see. That day, three hundred Russian newspapers paid tribute to Anna Politkovskaya, not caring at all about displeasing or contradicting a president who said she had little influence. They published a selection of Anna's articles. Astonished Russians who'd known nothing about her suddenly discovered her. That day, I took no fish home but instead a huge armful of newspapers. Then Vera's daughter was born. She was named Anna, like the grandmother she came so close to knowing.

Since then, I've lost my dear friend Natalya Estemirova, who often worked with Anna. Natalya was part of Memorial and wrote in the *Novaya Gazeta*. She was abducted one morning when she left her home, and then murdered. Now, six people work secretly in Chechnya for the *Novaya Gazeta* and send information. All women.

Since then, the newspaper has conducted its own investigation into Anna's murder, helping justice to move forward.

Since then, the families of the *Nord-Ost* victims, whom Anna often met with, are daring to fight the government, demanding accountability, and never failing to pay tribute to her on their website.

Since then, the mothers of Beslan, whom Anna advised, have courageously referred their case to the European Court of Human Rights to find out the truth about their children's deaths.

Since then, on websites, blogs, and social networks, people tell their true stories directly, and the powers-that-be cannot—not yet anyway—put a stop to this kind of free expression.

Since then, every October 7, someone comes to pick me up and take me to Chistoprudny Boulevard, five minutes away from the *Novaya Gazeta*. Every year a mixed crowd of people gathers there in Anna's memory.

Today is December 24, 2011. For the second time in a month, nearly a hundred thousand people are lining the streets of Moscow to demand honest and fair elections. It is fourteen degrees, there is every kind of group and all sorts of flags, music and shouting, and so many young people with no experience of the Soviet Union, or even *perestroika*. Even we are astonished to see there are so many of us. The old bridge over the Moskva trembles beneath our feet. Nothing has been won, I know. When was the last time that happened? 1991. I miss Anna's hand at my side. I miss her words too, the ones she tirelessly spoke to the Russian people.

Afterword: They Too Said No

It's all right to be afraid. It's very useful, very normal. Doesn't fear warn us of imminent danger? Doesn't it sometimes prevent us from taking unnecessary risks?

Yet other types of fears also exist; they start out small and then grow. Some can begin in a playground, when one kid rules over thirty-five square yards and you stay silent in the face of an injustice. These fears follow you into the workplace, where you give in so you don't get a bad rap. And, of course, sometimes you're afraid because you're told to be afraid.

Did Anna Politkovskaya never feel fear? On the ground during the Chechen war she was extremely cautious,* and at the end of her book *A Russian Diary* she asks the question: am I afraid? Her answer is yes, very much so. But she also writes that she had to choose between several fears. The greatest of all was for the future of her country, where her children would live with the grandchildren she never knew. And like many of the journalists we'll talk about, she wasn't a war correspondent and didn't die among bunkers and bullets. Instead she died on her way home from the supermarket because of the "power of words" in which she believed. Fourteen years later, the president of the Philippines, Rodrigo Duterte, publicly threatened the life of Maria Ressa, director of the Rappler news site. Addressing her team, she echoed Politkovskaya's sentiment: "We must fear fear." A former CNN correspondent,

---

* Chechnya, a small republic in the Caucasus, has always contested Russian federal control. When the USSR was dissolved, it declared itself independent. The First Chechen War broke out in 1994 and ended in a very fragile peace in 1996. In 1999, an even more terrible war resumed. Anna Politkovskaya was reporting on it at a time when very few journalists were able to enter Chechnya.

Maria Ressa was the joint laureate of the 2021 Nobel Peace Prize.

"Yes, we growl and bite. Yes, we have sharp teeth and strong grip," said Dmitry Muratov, speaking about journalists. Rather aggressive talk for a Nobel Peace Prize winner!

In December 2021, a Nobel Prize like no other was awarded: for the first time, it recognized two journalists in the context of a global threat to freedom of the press. Dmitry Muratov is the editor of one of Russia's last remaining independent newspapers, *Novaya Gazeta*.

Anna Politkovskaya would have smiled to hear him talk about growling and biting. When it came to baring his teeth, her boss never held back. She also knew how to bite. But she wasn't there that day. Nor were Igor Domnikov, Yuri Shchekochikhin, the joyful libertarian Anastasia Baburova, the newspaper's young lawyer Stanislav Markelov, or its much-loved Chechnya correspondent Natalya Estemirova. Six of

Novaya Gazeta's collaborators had been assassinated.

In 1993, in the early days of the newspaper, people could drop by, walk in, walk out, talk in the open. Those were carefree, if not peaceful, years. For a long time now, people have had to pass a checkpoint to enter *Novaya Gazeta*'s premises. And the first thing visitors see is a white corridor lined with portraits of the dead. Beyond that, it's a hive of activity.

Standing in Oslo's grand and gilded city hall, Dmitry Muratov briefly evoked the past. The long lineage of Russian rebels, writers, and militants who, starting with the late nineteenth-century socialists known as the Decembrists,* paid for their ideas and words with years of exile in Siberia or confinement in fortresses, and often with their lives. The renowned writer Fyodor Dostoevsky was among those imprisoned for

---

* A group of officers, writers, and poets inspired by the French Revolution who, on December 14, 1825, attempted a coup against Tsar Nicolas to obtain numerous reforms and the end of serfdom.

associating with a group of utopian socialists. Aside from a brief period of freedom following the revolution of 1917, the Communist regime turned out to be even more severe, veering into terror with the rise of Joseph Stalin. Millions of people were sent to gulags—labor camps mostly located in Siberia—with little chance of survival. After Stalin's death, the regime relented, but it was still almost impossible to publish freely or to speak without fear. So dissidents appeared. Their texts circulated in the form of clandestine books known as *samizdat*.

Among the dissidents, Dmitry Muratov wanted to pay tribute to one of the most well-known: the physicist Andrei Sakharov, who won the Nobel Peace Prize in 1975 but was prevented from leaving the USSR. It was no coincidence. Sakharov had co-founded the NGO Memorial. This organization has not only collected a historical treasure trove of testimonies and life stories from the Stalinist period, but has also always been involved in the fight for human rights. It is thus very critical of Putin's power. Fifteen days after the 2021 Nobel Prize ceremony, Memorial was dissolved after being condemned as a "foreign agent," a sad echo of Stalin's "enemy of the people." But in the videos filmed in front of the Palace of Justice, youthful faces proclaim: "We will not disappear." Perhaps that is the lesson we can take from this: in a country where successive powers seek to destroy freedom of thought, opponents always emerge. Whether their name is Pussy Riot or Alexei Navalny.*

But it was not only to Russia that Dmitry Muratov spoke in December. It was to all of us. "The world has fallen out of love for democracy. The world has become disappointed with the power elite. The world has begun to turn to dictator-

---

* A political opponent of Vladimir Putin, Alexei Navalny came up with an electoral tactic to defeat him, was poisoned while on campaign, and saved from the brink of death in a German hospital. Knowing he would be arrested on his return to Russia, he chose to go back and publish an indictment-documentary online against Putin and his "palace." He is currently being detained in harsh conditions.

ship. We've got an illusion that progress can be achieved through technology and violence, not through human rights and freedoms. This is progress without freedom? It is as impossible as getting milk without having a cow. . . . 'Are you not afraid?' is the most common question my colleagues get. . . . We are the antidote against tyranny." He ended his speech by saying, "I want journalists to die old."

Journalism has indeed become a high-risk profession, whether the journalists work for a paper, TV channel, news agency, or blog. In twenty years, more than sixteen hundred journalists have died while pursuing their work. In 2021, according to Reporters Without Borders, forty-six journalists were killed and nearly five hundred imprisoned, 20 percent more than the previous year. This was, of course, the result of the coup in Myanmar, with its series of arrests and repression that affected everyone, including the independent press. It was the result of ongoing demonstrations by Belarusians against the autocrat Lukashenko and his twenty-six-year reign. And it was the result of China's policies. With 127 reporters and bloggers detained, its domestic policy has earned it the title of "the world's largest prison for journalists." Its foreign policy is also to blame: while China had pledged to respect the tradition of a free press in Hong Kong, 2021 was a year of subjugation. The *Apple Daily* newspaper folded, its founder Jimmy Lai was arrested and is now threatened with life imprisonment. Six months later, Stand News was shut down and part of its team arrested along with several bloggers. All were reporting on the large-scale pro-democracy movement.

Maria Ressa could also have evoked a litany of deaths as she received her Nobel Peace Prize. Two days before her departure for Oslo, Jess Malabanan, who worked for various international media in the Philippines, was shot dead. His was the sixteenth assassination since Duterte came to power. But Maria Ressa chose instead to warn us against another danger. Internet giants, she said, "make more money by spreading that hate" and "bringing out our fears." They let "toxic sludge" course through our information system. After all, a click is a click. Mobbed with disinformation and targeted attacks, her news site, Rappler, did the math: with twenty-six fake Facebook accounts you can influence three million people. But the internet also offers salvation.

Without the internet, who would have known that Avinash Jha, a young reporter from a remote Indian province, had been burned alive for his investigation into illegal clinics? Who would have followed the fate of Narges Mohammadi, "the voice of imprisoned Iranians," herself behind bars once again? Of Le Trong Hung and Pham Doan Trang, among forty-three other journalists imprisoned in Vietnam? Of reporter Zhang Zhan, on a hunger strike after a year in jail for covering the pandemic in China? Of Hisham Abdelaziz, losing his eyesight in a prison in Cairo, Alia Awad, suffering from tumors in another Egyptian jail cell, or Mohamed Oxygen, the blogger who attempted suicide? Or even of Alaa Abd el Fattah, another blogger, in and out of prison since 2006 for his opposition to the government and the Muslim Brotherhood? Latin America, Africa, Asia—no region is exempt. Not even the United States or Europe, although they are impacted to a far lesser degree.

Carrying on the work is normal too. In the Mediterranean, the tiny island of Malta has five hundred thousand inhabitants and a strong reputation for rampant corruption. Since 2008, on her personal blog, Daphne Caruana Galizia had been publishing the results of multiple (and widely read) investigations into corruption and the Maltese government's questionable passport sales. On October 16, 2017, she fell victim to a car bomb. Her sister and her son Matthew have been moving heaven and earth to ensure that those responsible are found and sentenced. Matthew and forty-five other journalists from fifteen countries are continuing her investigations. As a result of this, and following numerous citizen demonstrations, the prime minister was forced to resign, and the alleged contractor of the murder, the businessman Yorgen Fenech, was arrested.

At the *Novaya Gazeta*, Elena Milashina, who initially intended to work in cultural journalism, pestered Dmitry Muratov until he let her go to Chechnya to follow in the footsteps of Anna Politkovskaya and Natalya Estemirova. Elena Kostyuchenko, who arrived in Moscow at seventeen from the town of Yaroslav, became an intern at the paper after reading an article by Anna Politkovskaya, "a revelation of what journalism can be." She is now a reporter and investigator like Anna, who ventures into difficult terrain, and on top of that fights for gay rights, receives awards, and participates in conferences in the United States.

NGOs like Reporters Without Borders, or more recently the Committee to Protect Journalists, identify, intervene, and question leaders who often favor trade contracts over human rights. They recently created a People's Tribunal in The Hague to investigate the murders of journalists (80 percent of which remain unsolved). They set up the Journalism Trust Initiative to thwart fake news. Forbidden Stories gives a platform to news investigations that can't always be published where they were carried out, and pursues stories from investigative journalists who were murdered. Journalists team up across borders to organize joint publications. They create a network against fear.

Many of those who were murdered or remain in prison were widely read or watched. Their job was to report, reveal, respect reality, and share their views. Simply to tell us what's going on. The rest is up to us, readers.

Chronology

1978: Anna Mazeppa, a student, marries Sasha Politkovski, also a student. A few months later their first child, Ilya, is born.

1980: Anna Politkovskaya graduates with a degree in journalism.

1985: Mikhail Gorbachev, General Secretary of the Communist Party, launches a policy of economic, political, and cultural liberalization with *perestroika* and *glasnost*.

1986: On April 26, a reactor at the Chernobyl nuclear power plant explodes.

1989: The Berlin Wall falls.

1991: The end of the USSR is proclaimed. Gorbachev resigns and Yeltsin is elected. Chechnya declares its independence.

1994: The First Chechen War begins.

1996: In July, Boris Yeltsin is re-elected.

1999: Boris Yeltsin appoints Vladimir Putin, head of the FSB, as prime minister. Anna Politkovskaya starts working at the *Novaya Gazeta*. On August 31, the first attack on Chechnya begins in a series that leaves more than three hundred dead and thousands injured. The Second Chechen War begins.

2000: In February, Grozny falls. In March, Vladimir Putin is elected with over 50 percent of the vote.

2001: Anna Politkovskaya receives the Golden Pen Prize of the Russian Union of Journalists and the Amnesty International Global Award for Human Rights Journalism.

2002: On October 23–26, the Moscow theater hostage crisis occurs. On the twenty-sixth at dawn, the Russian special forces diffuse gas in the theater. The victims number 170.

2004: Vladimir Putin is re-elected with 70 percent of the vote.

On September 1, the Beslan school hostage crisis in Ossetia: 344 dead, including 186 children. Anna Politkovskaya is a victim of poisoning. The same year, she shares the Olof Palme Prize with Lyudmila Alexeyeva and Sergei Kovalev, two former dissident members of Memorial, as well as receiving the Vázquez Montalbán International Journalism Award.

2005: In March, the Chechen president-elect

and guerrilla leader Aslan Maskhadov is killed by Russian forces.

2006: On October 7, Anna Politkovskaya is found shot dead in the elevator of her apartment building in Moscow.

2007: In November Ramzan Kadyrov, a former leader of the Chechen security service, becomes prime minister of Chechnya, supported by Vladimir Putin.

2009: In January, Stanislav Markelov and Anastasia Baburova are murdered in public. In July, Natalya Estemirova is kidnapped and killed. All three worked for the *Novaya Gazeta*.

2014: Anna Politkovskaya's murder goes to trial: a former Russian policeman and three Chechen mercenaries are sentenced, but no contractor. Russia annexes Crimea (Ukraine), triggering European sanctions.

2015: Opposition leader Boris Nemtsov is murdered, setting off mass protests in Moscow.

2020: Alexander Lukashenko is re-elected in Belarus. The election is highly contested, with demonstrations throughout the country. Five hundred journalists are arrested.

2021: More than fifteen Belarusian journalists are still detained. They are often given harsh sentences of up to eighteen years in prison on various pretexts.

December 10, 2021: Journalists Dmitry Muratov and Maria Ressa receive the Nobel Peace Prize.

December 27, 2021: Gulag historian Yuri Dmitriev is sentenced to fifteen years in prison after a fabricated trial.

December 28, 2021: The Russian Supreme Court dissolves the NGO Memorial.

For More Information

BOOKS:
Is Journalism Worth Dying For?: Final Dispatches, by Anna Politkovskaya
Putin's Russia: Life in a Failing Democracy, by Anna Politkovskaya
A Russian Diary, by Anna Politkovskaya
Gomorrah: A Personal Journey into the Violent International Empire of Naples' Organized Crime System, by Roberto Saviano
In the Country of Men, by Hisham Matar
Comradely Greetings: The Prison Letters of Nadya and Slavoj, by Slavoj Žižek and Nadya Tolokonnikova
Read & Riot: A Pussy Riot Guide to Activism, by Nadya Tolokonnikova

VIDEO AND FILM:
Summer Palace, by Lou Ye
Putin's Palace, by Alexei Navalny, published online

following his arrest: www.youtube.com/
watch?v=mMxqTae75Fs
A Thousand Cuts, by Ramona Diaz on Maria Ressa
Conference, by Ivan I. Tverdovsky
"Murder in Malta" on Daphne Caruana Galizia:
youtube.com/watch?v=9ywojofqtX0

LINKS:

Forbidden Stories: forbiddenstories.org
Hold the Line for Maria Ressa: betc.com/en/socit/hold-
the-line1
Reporters Without Borders: rsf.org/en
Committee to Protect Journalists: cpj.org/2021/12/
number-of-journalists-imprisoned-around-the-
world-sets-new-record
Journalism Trust Initiative: journalismtrustinitiative.org
International Memorial: memo.ru/en-us/memorial/
mission-and-statute
Novaya Gazeta: novayagazeta.ru/articles/2021/11/30/
russia-explained
Amnesty International: amnesty.org
Elena Kostyuchenko at Hunter College: youtube.com/
watch?v=ikFJKVJy3zA
Elena Kostyuchenko, "Russia's Propaganda War":
youtube.com/watch?v=bazDuUJ9RCQ